Exceptional Date

Paranormal, dark eroctica, romance, fairy tales story

Lana Kendra

it wasn't bought for your personal use only, go back to
your favorite ebook retailer and buy your copy. Thank you
for acknowledging this author's efforts.

Table of Contents

Content Warning

Due to its sexual content, this book is only for those over the age of legal adulthood. There are some topics with a lot of foul language. All of the characters are at least eighteen years old.

Introduction

Are you in search of an exciting and thrilling book to read? Look no further than this extensive collection of Erotic Suspense book. I offer a wide range of genres, including Romantic Erotica, Fantasy, and Urban BDSM Fiction, to cater to even the most discerning reader. Whether you enjoy Anthologies, Westerns, or Paranormal Romance, I have something to suit your taste. My collection also includes Poetic Folklore, Interracial, Black & African American Literary Criticism, and Gothic Horror for those who crave a deeper and darker reading experience. If you're interested in Futuristic, LGBTQ+, Short Stories, or Lesbian literature, my diverse range of options will keep you captivated. Additionally, I offer Humorous, Victorian, New Adult, and College Women's Psychological Mysteries for those seeking a lighter but equally engaging read. Furthermore, My Fairy Tale Collections,

Transgender, Contemporary Western, Bisexual, and Poetry genres will transport you to different worlds and explore a variety of themes. For my Teen and Young Adult readers, I have a selection of European Geography, Cultures, eBooks, Loners, Outcasts, Mythology, Folk Tales, and much more. With such a wide array of options to choose from, you'll never run out of thrilling and enchanting stories to immerse yourself in.

It is important to emphasize that this content is exclusively intended for individuals who are 18 years of age or older.

Exceptional Date

Under the neon glow of the lights, in a busy amusement park, a man and a woman stood by a machine and observed people playing. Or, it seemed, they were observing. As it was, they were just staring at one other.

She occasionally looks. He occasionally looks. Strangely though, their gazes never once met.

A year ago, Stacy and Austin crossed paths in their school's bustling hallways. Amid the nervous banter of young, inexperienced freshmen, they clicked right away. They came from distinct buddy circles and were both shy individuals.

But when they spoke to each other, words came naturally to them. After orientation, the two would often exchange glances and welcomes from across the room for the next few weeks.

Luckily, their classes were the same. Stacy would

frequently catch herself glancing at Austin's back during free periods.

Sure, he had a beautiful appearance, but it was his kind disposition that truly caught her attention. She was certain that she had never encountered someone with such sensitivity.

Austin was also compelled to take notice of her. Everyone attends the school.

Nevertheless, he was aware that she was different from the others in some way. Perhaps her inner strength. The kind of quiet that learned early in life that she didn't have to be loud to be understood.

That and her seemingly boundless charm, anyway.

Stacy appeared to be the ideal poster child for the ideal poster family, resembling one of those glossy celebrity family publications his mother peruses.

Green eyes and blonde hair. He was slightly taller than the

other person, only a few inches in front.

very simple and unpretentious. incredibly bright, albeit a touch sheltered.

She was fortunate to have wealthy parents who were involved in her life—you would be shocked at how uncommon that is.

She also looked well-groomed. Even though she was studying in psychology alongside Austin, she had excellent fashion sense, which helped her achieve her goal of becoming a cosmetologist. Austin, however, had no knowledge of fashion.

She gets along with everyone, more than that. He refers to everyone, too. She was the person you went to if you wanted anything from a faculty member or the club.

With everything going on, Austin was unable to take his gaze off of her.

He had no idea that the emotion was reciprocated.

Until they met each other, their eyes would constantly dart across rooms. Their pals eventually found out what was going on before they did.

It wasn't until several months later that they began to realize it themselves. It was on the Fourth of July. The campus was as much decked with blue, white, and red hues as it was with people.

at an attempt to escape the chaos, the two ended up collaborating on a project at the library.

Possibly the most demanding and fulfilling experience Austin has ever had.

It was all too much—the constant flirting in spite of their butterflies in their stomachs, the words hanging in the air since neither of them dared to express their sentiments. It was made much worse by the sporadic stillness.

Stacy gained the confidence she needed when the few individuals still inside the library eventually left.

Her heart was pounding, but she inquired in a quiet, steady voice, "Hey, can I tell you something?"

Austin raised his head and made eye contact with her for the first time that day. "Yeah, sure."

Despite the complete silence in the room, she said, "I've liked you for a long time," in a scarcely audible voice.

His mouth fell. "Cum again?"

Stacy gave him a serious look and burst out laughing. His expression was so precious.

"Is this a joke? Because it's not a very funny joke," said Austin.

She gave a headshake.

"I'm not joking. I've liked you for a long time — and I heard from my friends that you might like me a little too. Is that true?" she inquired.

Austin shook his head after needing a minute to recover

from his disbelief.

"I don't."

Looked down, Stacy looked unhappy, "Oh..."

"I like you a lot."

She looked up into his gaze once more and then rolled her eyes. "You know, you could've just said yes."

Austin honestly answered, "I'm sorry. I just had to make sure you knew how much I liked you."

She blushed a lot after that, boy.

After then, it was much simpler for them to speak.

The honesty of their feelings brought them comfort and calm in the middle of the silence that made them ponder more loudly and the sporadic giddy laughter. At last, the words that had been unsaid for the last few months were said.

Their initial unease gradually subsided as well, to be

replaced with this... tangible excitement. They came to understand their common interests, their convictions, and what gets them out of bed in the morning.

As the days stretched into weeks and those weeks into months, their relationship only got closer. A month ago, they made the decision to attempt dating.

On their third date, Stacy and Austin seemed to have found a little balance, relaxed, and just the two of them in this neon world of casual whimsy. This was in contrast to the first two dates, where there was a lot of pressure to make it romantic.

She looked around at the group of people gathered and observed, "It's getting a little hot in here. We should go somewhere else." Really, that was understandable. The men in front of them are extremely skilled at shooting those golden hoops.

The partner gave a nod. "Okay."

Kids laughing filled the theme park as Stacy guided Austin by the hand and threaded her way through the throng.

She was used to handling pandemonium because she grew up with four wild elder brothers.

The only time they stopped harassing the two was when the sun actually set and Austin had to leave, particularly when she welcomed him to the house for the first time.

Luckily, her brothers' buddy Warren held them back a bit. He was a senior at her school as well, although he was majoring in business. As a result, he didn't spend much time with Austin.

She was startled out of her reverie when she sensed her boyfriend assuming the initiative. "Hey, let's go there. I want to get you something."

She followed his gaze as it lingered on the crane. Although she had never been particularly fond of plush animals, the idea of receiving one from him made her heart skip a beat.

The man guided her to the machine and put some coins in with a calm hand.

"Do you have anything you like here?"

"Not really..."

Before she could finish her sentence, Stacy's gaze locked on a yellow Minion in the upper left corner. Could it be that Bob?

Austin laughed, following her eyes, "I figured as much."

She pouted at him and elbowed his chest. "And what's that supposed to mean?"

He smiled. "I'm just saying you don't exactly have the most normal taste."

The claw moved in accordance with his will, trying to grab the simple yellow plush toy without spending any more time.

It managed to seize hold of the body, but the soft toy

dropped before it could be lifted up because of the weak grasp.

"That's okay, Tin. We should go. Everyone knows these claw machines are a scam."

Her pulse skipped a beat when a grin pushed past the man's lips. "Let's just try two more times, okay?"

She gave a vacant nod.

When Austin tried again, it didn't work. Now she could tell he was getting a bit impatient.

In an attempt to defuse the situation, she remarked, "That was actually better than the last. I'm impressed."

His final opportunity, he joked, and inserted another coin. Surpassing both of them's expectations, Austin succeeded on the third try.

"Yes!" with a grin.

With a gleam in her eyes, Stacy shouted, "No freaking way!

I can't believe you did that. I've never seen anyone win at these!"

He gave her a quick glance and removed the soft toy before offering it to her. "It's all thanks to the way you were looking at me," he replied.

A pink glow spread across Stacy's cheeks. She laughed and took his hand.

"Well, in that case, I'll take the credit. Teamwork, right?"

As they made their way toward the rides, their lighthearted conversation filled the air. Typical draws, actually. There's a rollercoaster, a teacup ride, bumper cars, and a ferris wheel that's roughly 80 feet above the ground.

"You want to ride that? The line is a little long, but it should be fun."

She examined the line. To say that Little was understated.

"Yeah, of course. That sounds great. Let's go."

The rollercoaster seemed more like her thing, if she was being honest. She cherished the feeling of excitement. Very exciting.

However, she has never gone on a ferris wheel ride with a man.

She really loved experiencing it; it's like one of those corny couple things you see in movies and literature.

So she consented.

With their fingers still entwined, the two made their way over to the ferris wheel. But just as they were ready to form a queue,...

The phone vibrated for Stacy. A text was sent.

She read it cover to cover.

Austin was too preoccupied with the line to notice the change in her demeanor.

He didn't notice something was wrong until she gently

touched his shoulder.

"Hey, um, could we maybe reschedule a bit? I believe it's the ice cream, but my stomach feels a little off.

With a look of worry in his eyes, he nodded. "Yeah, obviously! Do you require a companion?"

"Nah, nie! I'm doing great. Only... Are you okay with waiting here?"

Actually not. For us, I could hold the line."

She nodded, as though in a little daze; her eyes were darting, obviously fixed on something else.

"Hey, what's the deal?"Austin took her shoulders in his hands and met her eyes.

Stacy looked back, then leaned in to plant a kiss on him— just her lips meeting his, nothing more, meant to be innocent.

However, it didn't feel that way at all.

The boyfriend wasn't sure what it was exactly that made him shudder, but there was definitely something odd about this kiss.

They parted their lips as she said, "It's not much. Okay, I'll be back shortly."

With a smile on her face, she gave Austin a nod; he remained mute after the kiss.

He had little time to consider it further because his stunning girlfriend had already turned around and was leaving the ferris wheel and him behind.

The boyfriend dismissed it, figuring it was simply him being a horndog.

Stacy ran to the bathroom, her heart pounding out of her chest.

It was peculiar, though, that she chose to use the women's restroom on the right rather than the men's on the left.

No, this wasn't an accident; Stacy deliberately went into

the men's restroom after making sure no one was looking.

She pulled at her blazer, desperate for some warmth as the chilly air blasted her figure from every direction. She was already missing Austin.

But ideas were forbidden around him, especially those involving Austin.

She looked at the man in front of her; he appeared to be waiting for someone as he leaned carelessly on one of the stalls.

The man in front of her was the true reason she fled.

"Hi, why did it take you so long? I believed you had betrayed me."

She pouted at him and said, "Warr, I told you not to call me when I'm on a date."

He laughed, saying, "Sorry, Stace. All I really need to do right now is empty my balls. You do realize what I mean? Can you believe I haven't had sex in two days?"

Stacy blushed; she didn't have to imagine. She'd only done it six times with Austin so far, which works out to about once a month on average.

In actuality, since she became eighteen, she has exponentially more sex with this guy.

Her first... and second... was Warren.

Fourth, Fifth, and Third.

She was scarcely able to count anymore.

The reason her physique is so... is his fault.

"After seeing one of our videos, Becca's boyfriend abruptly canceled. However, I'm quite convinced he's a closet cuck. It will definitely work out.

"Warr, what are you trying to say? that I'm a reserve? I'm amazed by you!"

Becca thought, "This guy's nerve. She's much better than that bitch."

The girlfriend shook her head, but what exactly was causing her anger?

Warren glanced at her and smiled softly, tucking her hair behind her ears, as if he could see what she was thinking. "Oh, Stace. Do you harbor envy?"

She tightened her teeth and replied, "You're insane."

Warren kissed her cheeks and said, "You don't have to act fake around me. I will not think any less of you if we forgo this phony act for your lover. Still, I like my females to be envious. What justification did you offer what's-his-name now?"

"Oh, here we go again!" was her new outburst at his insolence. Warr, one year has passed! You could be a little troubled to recall his name, Austin."

He mumbled, obviously not listening, "Yeah, yeah," as he inspected her body appropriately.

Under the man's (admittedly) stunning eyes, Stacy always

felt like a product to be evaluated, her physique and curves reduced to statistics, and she shuddered.

She never really felt it with Austin, even if their eye colors were too close.

"Also, do you possess a condom?" He said, "Left mine back at the house."

Though she knew the answer, Stacy was hesitant to provide it.

Wayne smiled.

"You do."

"Talk less! That is not how it is.

How was it back then, Stace? Because it's not for your narcissistic lover at all."

"It. observed it in the home... and I took hold of it just in case. Nothing more, please."

"So why do you appear embarrassed?"He made a funny

point.

That's because Stacy remained stoic, unwilling to look up into his critical eyes.

Warren, however, gave her a quiet glance before planting a kiss on her earlobes. "Don't be. I adore girls who are ready.

She shouldn't have been excited from his comments, but she was. His intimacy never truly helped.

Her body leaned in and kissed him back, her hands instinctively creeping towards his lower body like a magnet.

The bathroom may be empty right now, but Warren couldn't guarantee no one would come in. He could only hope people would get the idea and leave. "Someone's excited," he whispered teasingly before he pushed her against the door, cornering her inside one of the stalls.

At least on Stacy's behalf.

Warren began to nibble at her neck and caress her tits, making Stacy groan in the process. The man smiled at the look of confusion on her face.

Though Stacy preferred to act otherwise, she has always been a hard-core; since her first, almost nothing has been off-limits, and he wondered whether she felt it was his fault.

Because he would definitely deny it. Stacy was an A-class pervert from the moment he met her.

She stared him up like a piece of candy every time he came around, regardless of the fact that her brothers were standing right in front of her.

She most likely assumed he was unaware of the sly, lewd looks that came from those stunning green eyes.

But he did, and for months it drove him insane.

Ultimately, he was unable to restrain himself, primarily due to realizing he didn't have to.

Twirling her hair and flirting with him while her brothers aren't looking, the harlot clearly desired it and enjoyed being recognized as a woman.

He knew she would be thrilled to feel even more like one.

Warren, therefore, swept her off her feet and fucked her like a lady one day when he discovered no one was home.

In her room, followed by her brother's.

Warren felt he had met his equal at that very instant.

He probably would have said yes if she had offered to date him, and he would have quickly dumped his fuck pals.

But she refrained.

Yes, she did call him out on a daily basis, but she never once showed her interest in that manner.

Gently, "Give us a kiss, Stace," he instructed.

And now this twisted game of jealousy and control was all he could do.

It was looking like a fantastic date with her boyfriend too, so she nodded and unbuckled him with aplomb. She really should get back to Austin ASAP. This man had a lot of nerve treating her like a second choice.

She was not sure which of those two infuriated her more.

Warren was a monster, but Stacy kept forgetting that until he shoved his cock down her throat; over three times as big as Austin, she assumed Warren was just like the other guys because he was her first. Nevertheless, she opened her mouth and welcomed him.

When she discovered that Austin, and most males in general, don't have nearly as much as Warren was carrying, it was quite a shock.

"Oh my god. Stace, your mouth feels wonderful. The first time, you could hardly take in three inches. In the first minute, you're already deepthroating nearly half of my cock. Jesus, it seems like they grow up so quickly."

He kissed his lips and gave her a gentle head rub.

The nostalgic expression on his face made her smile.

Warren moved her hair softly to the back, then abruptly changed his style, thrusting his hips while holding her head with both hands, and before she knew what was going on, he was smoothly fucking her mouth.

As though she were a magnificent specimen of a fleshlight.

"Oh my god. Screw me! Yes, right there! I see, Stace. You are the greatest! Pull the back in even more, huh? Fuck that!"

Stacy bobbed her head on Warren's entire length, feeling lightheaded and increasingly as though the world was spinning around her and the only way to stay alive was to take in his cock and pray that a tiny bit of oxygen came along with it.

She pondered what would happen if her parents and brothers saw her like this—their picture-perfect young girl getting her throat ripped like a pro.

Their prim and proper Stacy breathing in the cock of their best friend, her school senior, as if she were infatuated with it.

Everything in Stacy's life always seemed less significant to her while she was with Warren; she felt like a phony. This included her temperament and principles.

She was unable to defend or even understand why.

The pull she felt for him was stronger than any narcotic she had ever read about.

He had completely destroyed her, to the point where she consented to cheat on someone she truly loved on their romantic date.

Stacy thought blankly, "Maybe she should date him instead if she was going to be this easy."

No, that's absurd.

"Oh, Stace, screw you. I'm infatuated with your cock. I trained you so well, God."

He certainly did; after their first hook-up, Stacy never went a day without sucking him off, her small youthful body being the target of intense pounding and daily humiliation rituals from Warren.

She learned how to deepthroat, put her legs behind her head for him, ride him for an hour straight without getting tired, and even sucked the cum straight out of another girl's ass and passed it around with two other women like it was a sport. In the process, she even learned several things that most women even twice her age couldn't do.

He named it the Butt Nut Olympics.

She tried every sexual pose she saw in a pornographic film with him right away; in fact, he made her view and play out his favorite flicks.

She hated that she loved it, but eventually she came to love these short viewing sessions.

Actually, she enjoyed her dates with Austin almost as much as she did her time with Warren.

Nearly.

Warren pushed his cock deeper while she eased her throat, her gentle hands gripping his thighs.

He didn't pause until her lips were on the actual base of his cock, which allowed her to catch her breath.

"Whoa! Ah, fuck. Hey Stace, I'm all in. Baby, do you mind? Simply the norm."

She was aware of the standard.

Another thing she picked up from him was the art of simulating gagging. Since Stacy never really had a gag reflex, she never really knew how to do it, but Warren showed her how to make a fake one so she could squeeze her throat by inhaling.

Imagine kegel exercises for your mouth.

Her gaze shifted to him. Now, his massive cock was shoved all the way down her throat. She could feel it jabbing at the back of her windpipe, but there wasn't much resistance. As if her body concurred that this was how her throat was meant to be used.

At his suggestion, she nodded and swallowed. Her gorgeous green eyes began to well up with tears as she violently choked on his cock. It was difficult since you were unable to breathe freely.

She let go of some saliva, which eventually soaked the floor.

Before licking it off with his own tongue, Warren used his thumb to tenderly remove some of the saliva from the corners of her lips. "You're getting sloppy. Do it like I taught you, Stacy."

Before flicking her tongue on his testicles, she sucked in

her dripping saliva, causing bubbles and froth to form around her attractive lips. Warren's favorite section was this one.

The expression in her eyes while she does an act that her intellect knows is degrading.

She nevertheless does it cheerfully.

After taking his wet cock out of her clinging lips and smearing it all over her face, he gripped her chin.

Warren became glazed over the scene.

"Fuck. You're so pretty. My pretty little personal cocksucker, aren't you? You're making me feel so good, Stace — I love you! Please don't stop. I love you so much! Keep sucking, baby."

She kept slurring on his balls, and her eyes got moist. Don't say that, she silently told herself.

Say nothing of these kind words as you force me to do this.

Suddenly, Stacy's thoughts turned to her boyfriend. Austin was also gifted with language.

She questioned what he was doing at the moment.

She had no idea that Austin was still waiting in line. Like Stacy, he was wondering about his lover and thinking of her.

Clearly, he was unaware that the real question was not what to ask, but rather who.

A vendor came up to Austin and said, "Sir, would you be interested in buying some nuts?"

"Oh, sure. How much?"

Despite the vendo's questionable pricing, Austin decided to purchase a whole can. Although he didn't like them, he was very certain Stacy did.

Austin waited in line patiently, not realizing that his ideal girlfriend was currently sucking on her favorite nuts—two fat ones.

"Oh, what's this?"

With a pop, Warren took his knackers out of Stacy's mouth and gripped her chin. His fingers dug into her bag and produced... A plush yellow toy.

Stacy squirmed.

B*tch.

"This is the Bob-guy, right? I haven't watched it, but it's everywhere."

"Austin, he... won me that," she answered, sounding somewhat defensive.

He cocked an innocent head. "Really, that's... cute."

Still, Stacy doubted it was innocent. Because Warren's cock began twitching wildly as soon as he said that statement.

She was aware of his head tilt and the sparkle in his eyes. She scowled. He had the switch on.

With a tone that was almost imploring, Stacy pleaded, "Can you put it back?"

"Why are you talking? Stick your tongue out."

Stacy shut her jaw.

"I said," his eyes turned cold as he stressed every word, "Stick. You. Language. "Out."

When he's like this, Stacy can't fight him, so she gradually gave in and followed his instructions.

He said, "Thank you, Stacy," and then gave her a tongue-slap.

Furthermore, why should we return this? Alvin put a lot of effort into this. toy, did he not?"

She sighed and said, "His name's Austin."

She spoke incoherently and jumbledly because of her stuck-out tongue, but it didn't matter because he ignored her.

"So, do you believe he merits a small amount of recognition? It must be properly examined. Continue sucking.

Warren was just getting warmed up when he abruptly grabbed a grip of her hair and thrust his hips forward, burying more than half of his massive cock on her constricted throat. Stacy parted her mouth and feasted on the head of his enormous cock once more.

Even worse was when he held up the immaculate plush animal next to her while she struggled and really gagged, giving off the impression that they were both waiting for his verdict.

"I apologize!Stacy didn't see why she was apologizing; her partner had the right to give her a present. "She murmured, her mouth full of cock.

But she knew that the demon's rage could only be appeased by an apology.

His ruthless eyes, which bore a striking resemblance to her boyfriend's, seemed to hear her words and sneer at her.

Furious with desire, she turned away from him to stare at the memento of her date with Austin—the adorable small plush animal she had been overjoyed to get—watching her deterioration.

Made fun of, mocked, and tarnished since she was clearly beneath another man's massive cock, giving him her whole body in adoration.

This was a huge mistake.

Her hand darted between her legs as she was unable to contain herself any longer.

Upon observing her quivering physique and her groaning when his penis was in her mouth, Warren at last said, "You're so heartless, Stace..."

She was coldhearted, but for once, she consented.

Here she was, thoroughly debased by the award her

partner had earned for her, on her knees, feeling the guilt.

in the same manner as her.

"You're a fucking pervert, Stace, but I love you anyway...."

He patted her head tenderly and said, "Will he? If he was aware of your actions?"

Will Austin still love her if he knew she was this wicked and nasty? Even Stacy wasn't sure.

Her chest ached.

"I'm positive you too adore Alvin. I need you to be a good girl right now. Please look at the award he won for you and let me know if you believe you deserve it.He held out the soft toy and asked.

She was no longer sensible enough to correct Warren about her boyfriend's name.

Rather, Stacy turned cross-eyed and attempted to tilt her head to look directly at the soft toy, but her lips would not unwrap around Warren's manhood's base.

The way Austin's lips curled and his gaze met hers as he won the toy from the crane machine, she relived every aspect of that moment as if it were a scene out of a dream come true.

Even the sensation of her lips moving in favor of him.

except now she was speaking of nothing except the sounds of her devotion and a fat cock pressed firmly between her ruby lips.

Stacy could feel her brain preparing for a spine-tingling orgasm; she was about to cum.

Warren's smile and his wave of the plush toy in front of her face was what finally pushed her over the edge.

Stacy moaned, her legs trembling wildly from the fluids dripping over the ground.

Her orgasm took a minute to pass, and by the time she woke up, the plush toy was on the ground, half-soaked from her squirting, and Warren's dripping cock was laying on top of it, soaking her face as well.

Nothing smelled better than the man who owned you, so she inhaled his scent.

"I don't," was her response.

Stacy pulled out the condom she had brought, tore it open, put it in her mouth, and used a blowjob to put it on her senior's huge cock, as if to further demonstrate her lack of worth.

The man gave a tongue-click, continuing to be his favorite of her party tricks.

The sophomore could take no more waiting and got up, trampling on the plush toy she had been so glad to embrace the previous time she leaned on the stall and arched her back.

"Warr, fuck me already! Please, P! She pleaded, "Fuck me up, baby. I don't care which hole he went into as long as he fucks her really hard." She pushed her ass up towards him for easy access.

She was so unnaturally wet that it was leaking on his fingers, yet Warren still smiled and spread her pussy lips apart, swearing under his breath.

Warren penetrated her with a single motion while holding her waist, showing no signs of waiting for a guy.

Unconsciously, Stacy's eyes grew droopy as she finally felt the comforting curve of his cock embrace her.

Her entire body was happy.

"You're so incredibly tight, God. After spending time with him, you're this fucking tight all the time. Does it recognize his small dick and adjust itself automatically?Warren laughed in a mocking manner.

Gritting her teeth, Stacy said, "He's... No... fuck it. small...!"

Are you sure? Tell me, when he fucks you, where does the

youngster reach?"

Warren pinched her clit and then traced half the depth of his cock on her pussy with his finger.

"Okay... right here? Is he able to reach this far?"

Stacy was going crazy. Warren's disparaging remarks and the constant barrage of her pussy were overwhelming her with mind-numbing pleasure, and she could feel the familiar tingle of an orgasm flooding over her again.

"Oh no! He is unable to get there. He."

Stacy pushed, leading the man's fingers feebly.

"Look! He was... He's limited to reaching this far, oh, craaap."

"Shit. This little of a dick would keep me inside the fucking house forever. Hehe!"

Warren began beating her after raising her to a height where her toes hardly touched the floor.

Stacy shook with excitement, rolling her eyes as Warren struck all of her areas at once, making it impossible for her to understand what he was saying.

Stacy's world whirled around this passionate fucking, her toes curling as she forgot where she was or what she was doing before.

Was she out on some kind of date?

It is essentially irrelevant now.

"Stace, I'm about to cum. Do you want to join me in a cum?"

Indeed...! CUM ON YOUR BIG COCK, PLEASE! FUUUUCK, PLEASE LET ME CUM!"

"I want you to do something first."

True! Sure! WHATEVER, WARR! Just don't stop screwing me!"

Leaning her face into her forearms, Stacy pushed her body

back against Warren's powerful hips with such madness that she honestly didn't care if the stall collapsed at any moment and she was left naked in the bathroom.

Her toned legs were about to give out from the sheer pleasure of it; the only things keeping her from losing control were Warren's waist support and pure adrenaline.

"How about we do a video thank you for Alvin? He has shown you such kindness. Do you not believe he deserves it?"

Yeah! AWESOME BOYFRIEND!"Stacy turned to look at Warren, puckered her lips, and leaned in to give her a kiss.

Warren broke up the naughty tongue-wrestling for a minute as Stacy's wet tongue curled around his.

God, Stace, you kiss like fucking garbage!"

Though she presumably saw it in one of his favorite movies, she proudly showed him the obscene scene of their spit combining in her mouth, something he had never taught her.

"All right, grab the plush toy. It must be included in the video."

Warren whistled, really amazed, as Stacy fluidly snatched the fluffy Bob from the ground, keeping her ass elevated throughout his violent beating like a champ.

He could only imagine that she smiled at him, or at least in his direction, because she was having so much trouble focusing her eyes due to all of the mini-climaxes going on in her head.

With a smile on his face, the senior realized how much he enjoyed watching his spoilt sophomore daughter act out. Without pausing for thought, Warren pulled out his phone and began filming a selfie!

"Fuck!" he exclaimed. I apologize; I thought I was ready, but she feels like the greatest thing ever. Oooh, shit. Hi everyone, this is Warren. I'm the one watching. And that's"

"Hello, it's STAaaaACY — OOOOH!!!"""

"I apologize for that. She has a slight cock obsession."

To say little was an understatement, Stacy silently thought to herself.

The woman thrashed around and squealed in agreement, sounding like a pig. She even began to drool.

"HELLO! Warrell, I WUV YOUR COCK! HUGE COOOOCK WUV!"

She was astounded by how incredibly wonderful it felt.

In any case, this is a dedication to her boyfriend. Alvin. He's a lovely person, but he has this small prick that won't please this bitch. Today at the arcade, he won a reward for her, and I'm so happy that Stace is dating a little-dicked cuck who genuinely loves her!"

There was also a humorous understatement there, she realized.

Along with her thoughts, Stacy let out a loud gasp, "So little ~!"

She then demonstrated its tiny size to the camera with her thumb and index finger.

Warren adored it when she bashed her partner, and his lips curled smugly.

A unique message from your one and only is attached!"

Warren kept hitting her, yanking her hair and making her stare into the camera.

What have you got to say to your cuck, Stace?"

Glancing at her reflection on the screen, Stacy's pupils dilated, her vivid green irises resembling the subtly deepest recesses of the ocean, and sweat trickled from her furrowed eyebrows and out of her forehead.

Compared to how she had seemed at the start of the date, she appeared to be a complete disaster and insane.

Interestingly enough, having sex with Warren usually ends up like this: Stacy thinks about how far she's fallen and what actions she took to end up this way, followed by a brief but profound philosophical afterthought. It's as if one tick-tock feels like infinity stretched out.

Her mother trained her to always think for herself and select her own path; her father taught her that life is all about balance and discipline; her brothers encouraged her to search for the nicest men the world had to offer.

Her significant other, who demonstrated to her that love is what makes life worthwhile.

The concept of breaching every single one of the values they taught her with one guy shot like heroin into her head, causing her eyes to roll up as she squirted on her lover's cock.

"ALVIN, YOU ARE LOVED!" Oh my god, you are so beautiful! Arrr, I can't stop laughing! I appreciate you taking me out on this wonderful date today! Dear God, Baby, this is my favorite date with you! ~ I'm in love with the plush toy. FUCK, SHIT — MY PUSSY FEELS AMAZING! Sure, Oh! Yeah, WARR! I'M SLEEPING! Alvin, I'm CUUUUMMING AGAIN! Baby, this is for you! I am really excited to return from this place and ride the ferris wheel with you! I adore—"

Warren gave her cervix a harsh blow with his massive cock and came in a dazzling flash.

"JOKE! LOLOCK! OOOHHHH, MY PUSSY'S CUMMING SO MUCH!"Stacy felt the man filling up the condom inside of her, and as the world went white, a painful pleasure rushed through her body.

As Warren attempted to pull out, Stacy's pussy gripped on his cock like it didn't want to let go, causing him to gasp with unbelievable pleasure.

It took a few more minutes of mindless grunts before they

were finally able to ride out their collective tidal waves, but the condom slid right off his cock and got stuck in the tightness of her pussy. As soon as she felt him pull out, Stacy's legs collapsed and she dropped to the floor, her back still arched and her ass twitching.

Then nothing.

"It was that... fantastic," he eventually uttered in a tired voice.

She groaned in agreement and gave a happy, eager nod, her eyes closed. "Mmm...."

The part of her that comes out when she has sex with Warren never ceases to surprise her; she imagined acting in a movie scene would feel a lot like this; she knew the woman was her, yet at the same time, she didn't know her. Still reeling from the aftershocks, Stacy took a deep breath and slowly regained her edge.

There was no end to that woman's depravity; she was just

a bitch in heat with nothing but cock on her mind.

Ultimately, though, she was devoted to her family and to Austin as well.

Sex was only a once-in-a-while way to let out pent-up stress and lust—to let the other lady out.

The woman who is separated from the ideal little angel in her family.

An alter ego that sometimes seems too good to be true.

"Hey, do you hear me?" he asked her. The woman clearly wasn't hearing anything. With a chuckle, Warren pulled out the used condom and talked to the unmoving woman, "You should go going. Most likely, your guy is still waiting."

Stacy took a moment to register what he had said before she leapt to her feet, hurriedly tidying up her clothes and touching up her makeup.

"I hope to see you soon!"

Just as she was ready to leave, Warren said, "Wait."

"Yeah?" she asked, pausing to look at him."

He approached Stacy, savoring her sensual afterglow as he undid her skirt and fastened the used condom to the strings of her panties.

The man gave her a teasing smile and said, "Keep that right here, okay? Later evening, when you get home, we'll put on another one."

The idea of practically wearing another man's sperm while she went on her date with her lover made Stacy cringe.

really hot!

"Hold you at nine o'clock?"

She felt as though the excitement of today wouldn't end at this rate, so she nodded and gave him a passionate kiss.

She muttered, "You're going to be my last and my favorite amusement ride today— no matter what," and Warren smiled.

He said, "Go," and then smacked her in the butt.

She gave him a flirtatious grin before bolting from the bathroom to meet her boyfriend.

Austin was already the third person in line when she found him.

Her adorable partner turned around and gave her a wave, seemingly sensing her affectionate stare.

"Just in time, that is. So, you're doing better now, right?"

She nodded, thinking about how at ease she was feeling after several orgasms.

Fuck, before their dates now, she's probably going to want to fuck Warren.

He had destroyed yet another innocent object, and Stacy wondered whether she would ever get to live a really normal life.

The ferris wheel came to a standstill after a few minutes, and then it was their turn.

Austin said, "You first," and put out his arm to assist her. She grinned and got inside the cabin, and then the axle turned slowly and they took off together.

She whispered, "This view is incredible," in a tone that was gentle and full of wonder.

Indeed. Though it still doesn't compare to you, Austin said in a genuine tone, to which Stacy rolled her eyes and sneered, "Talker."

The guy laughed.

He said, "I had a great time tonight, Stacy," with loving eyes. I'm very happy we worked on this together."

"Me too, Tin," Stacy said, her heart thumping at his words as she rested on his shoulder. With your help, today has been wonderful."

She told herself she should thank Warren again tonight.

Their chat turned to dreams, passions, and shared hopes as the ferris wheel slid down slowly; each word strengthened their bond, creating an invisible crimson thread that connected them.

Austin hugged Stacy tightly as the ride came to a conclusion and said, "I don't want this night to end."

"Then let's make more moments like this," Stacy said, her fingers making circles on his hand as she nodded, her eyes matching his earnestness. "Together..."

Under the starry sky, Stacy and Austin made a pledge to each other that they would go on a lifetime of memorable dates while their hearts were enchanted with love.

Apart from the condom that was stuck to Stacy's panties and stuffed to the brim, everything seemed normal.

A symbolic condom fastened to the crimson thread of destiny.

It's so sensual, she thought.

She was eager to leave and go home after her time here.

Acknowledgments

The Glory of this book's success goes to God Almighty and my beautiful Family, Fans, Readers & well-wishers, Customers, and Friends for their endless support and encouragement.

About The Author

I've spent nearly a decade penning romantic novels. As a passionate writer of erotica, I craft dark, romantic erotica. Anime Naked Truth Se of Sacred Sexuality: Forbidden Seducing Short Stories of an Erotica Nude Sexy Girl Poster. Alongside Erotic Mystery Fiction, Victorian Erotica Sex, Black & African American Erotica, Euthanasia, Daddy Teaching, Forced Domination, Alpha Monster Cuckold, and BDSM for Adults, there's an Erotic Fiction in Kinky Family. I write dark, sensual romance because I adore the power of darkness and everything that it entails. Romance novels have always been my favorite kind of books, and now I'm writing them. The idea that you will like reading and enjoying my fiction as much as I enjoy pushing the frontiers of sexual pleasure in my writing thrills me more than anything else.